The Paraclete
TREASURY
of ANGEL
STORIES

Mary Joslin

Illustrated by Elena Temporin

PARACLETE PRESS
BREWSTER, MASSACHUSETTS

Angel of God, my guardian dear
To whom God's love commits me here,
Ever this day be at my side
To light and guard, to rule and guide.

Traditional

Contents

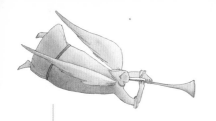

Choirs of Angels

*I*f you have heard
the sound of birdsong
in the morning air,
then you will know
that heaven's music
reaches everywhere.

I soar through the clear air
amazed at my own voice
and wondering if
there is an angel singing with me.

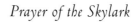

Prayer of the Skylark

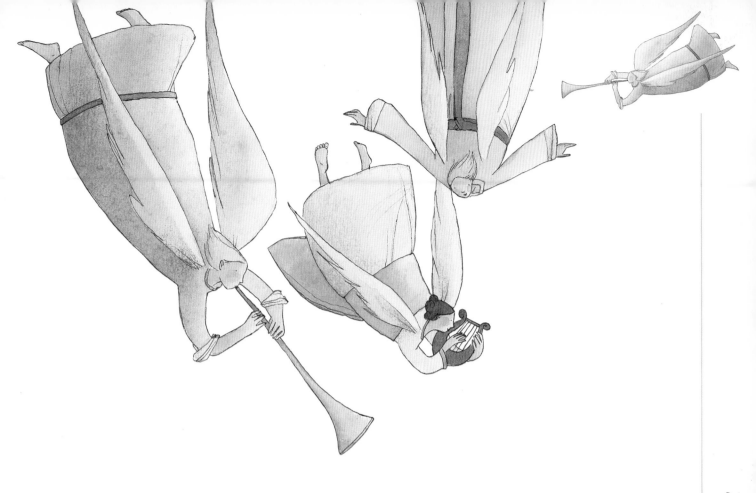

I don't feel afraid
to look up to the sky
and its miles and miles of blue;
for in the clear air
and the wide everywhere
is the love that surrounds me and you.

The Angel of Paradise

At the very beginning of all things, God planted a garden in Eden. Through the middle of the garden flowed a sparkling stream, and on its banks the trees grew strong and green. When their delicate and graceful blossoms fluttered to the ground, their fruits grew plump and round: apricots and apples, pomegranates and peaches, cherries and cherimoyas.

It was in this paradise garden that the first man and the first woman awoke.

'Look, Adam,' said God; 'Eve, come and see.' God's call rippled through the air like a warm and playful breeze. 'I have made all this for you to enjoy. All except that one tree, in the middle of the garden. Its fruit has the power to poison you and the whole world. If you eat it, all the good things you enjoy will be tainted with evil. You must not touch it.'

Adam and Eve had no need to go near the forbidden tree: everything God had given them was so very good.

One day, when Eve was sitting by herself, a strange creature came rustling through the leaves.

'What did God say you must not do?' it whispered.

Eve turned to see a snake-like head with eyes that glittered like jewels.

'We can do just about everything,' said Eve cheerfully. 'The only thing God warned us about was the tree over there in the middle of the garden. If we eat its fruit, it will poison us and the whole world with evil.'

'Did God really say that?' exclaimed the creature. 'What astonishing nonsense! You won't be poisoned: you will simply understand that there is evil as well as good, and then you will be wise – as wise as God, as it happens. Isn't it odd that God should want to deceive you!'

'Oh,' said Eve. She thought for a moment. 'It would be a good thing to be wise, wouldn't it?'

'Very good,' whispered the creature. 'You should have some fruit right away… and you should share it with that nice young man too.'

Eve reached up, plucked the golden fruit and took a bite. 'Mmm, very good,' she said. 'Adam, come and taste this.'

Not long after they had eaten, they felt their heads beginning to spin. 'Does the world look different to you?' asked Eve, trembling a little. 'Adam,' she whispered. 'We're naked. I never noticed before.'

'Come on,' said Adam. 'We can make clothes for ourselves. And then let's hide. We don't want God to find out what we've done.'

That evening, God came walking
through the garden, and God knew
what had happened. God spoke in a
voice that sent a chill frost through the air.
  'Now that you have tasted the poison of evil,
you cannot stay in this garden. You must go out
into the world where good and evil struggle side by
side, and where you will struggle to survive.'

Adam and Eve trudged out into a harsh world.
The air was cold, and the thorn bushes shivered in the wind.
They turned for one last, longing look at paradise.

God's own angel was standing there, silent and fierce. As they looked, the angel lifted a shining sword that slashed through the air like lightning. They turned away.

There was no way back to paradise.

The Stairway to Heaven

Among the descendants of Adam and Eve were two brothers. Their names were Esau and Jacob.

Esau was a hunter, tall and strong, with a flowing mane of red-gold hair.

Jacob, the younger, was slender and pale. He did not have the strength or the courage to go hunting, but he was devious and cunning. Little by little, he cheated Esau of all the rights of the firstborn son — first, the inheritance promised from their father; next, their father's blessing.

Esau's mood grew dark and angry. 'As soon as our father is dead, I shall kill the scoundrel with my own hands,' he threatened.

Their mother, Rebecca, was fearful of what might happen to her darling Jacob. She went to plead with her husband, Isaac.

'You must send Jacob to my brother's home, far away,' she urged him. 'He can find himself a wife from among my own kin there.'

Isaac agreed to the plan, and sent Jacob off.

It was a long and lonely journey, mile after weary mile. 'I have made myself a stranger to my own family,' Jacob sighed, as the sun's fire turned to smouldering ashes in the western sky. 'I even feel like a stranger to the God we worship.'

With these gloomy thoughts, he found a smooth stone on which to pillow his head and fell asleep.

In his dream he saw a vast stairway, tier upon tier of huge steps reaching up to heaven like a towering temple. It was thronged with angels, some coming down from heaven and others returning to it.

Then God came and spoke to him. 'I am going to make you the father of a great nation,' said God. 'Through your descendants, I will bless every nation of the world. I make this my solemn promise.'

At once, Jacob woke up. He rubbed his eyes. The vision had gone, but the words God had spoken were unforgettable.

'This place must be the gate that opens into heaven,' he whispered to the stars. In his heart, he knew that his descendants would open that gate for all the people in the world.

With new hope in his heart and his step, Jacob journeyed on.

Angels All Around

I go forth today
in the might of heaven,
in the brightness of the sun,
in the whiteness of snow,
in the splendour of fire,
in the speed of lightning,
in the swiftness of wind,
in the firmness of rock.
I go forth today
in the hand of God.

Irish prayer (8th century)

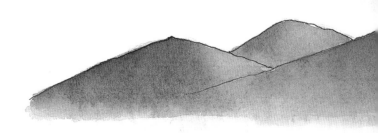

I walk with angels before me.
I walk with angels behind me.
I walk with angels above me.
I walk with angels around me.

Traditional

The Angel in the Flames

*K*ing Nebuchadnezzar of Babylon ruled a vast empire. He was rich, he was powerful, and he was dangerous.

When he gave the order for his officials to come to a great ceremony, every one of them obeyed.

They gathered on the wide plain outside the city and gazed in amazement at the sight that greeted them. There stood a huge golden statue, tall and menacing. Its metal eyes glinted fiercely in the sunlight; its gleaming lips were set in a permanent frown. This was the god Nebuchadnezzar had made: the god of a proud and cruel empire.

A herald stepped forward: 'People of all nations, all races, all languages. This ceremony will begin with the sound of trumpets and oboes, with lyres and zithers and harps. Then, when all the instruments join in, you must bow down to this gold statue that King Nebuchadnezzar has set up. Anyone who does not do so will be thrown into a blazing furnace. The fire is already burning.'

The music played. The people bowed down. They pressed their faces close to the ground, eager to smell the earth and not the bitter smoke that drifted over the plain.

Except for three young men: Shadrach, Meshach and Abednego. The guards seized them at once and dragged them to the king.

'We will not worship your statue,' they declared boldly. 'We are faithful to our own God. It may be that our God will save us from your blazing furnace and from your power. Even if he doesn't, we will not bow down to a lump of metal.'

King Nebuchadnezzar was furious: 'Make the fire seven times hotter,' he cried. 'Tie these men up and throw them into the heart of the flames.'

23

He watched with grim delight as Shadrach, Meshach and Abednego tumbled into the furnace. He was eager to hear the hissing and the sizzling as their flesh and their arrogance turned to ash.

Then his smile faded. 'I see four men walking in the fire,' he said anxiously. 'They are not tied up and they are not burning... and the fourth one...'

His voice faded away. Perhaps he had been mistaken, and there wasn't a fourth person. Perhaps it was just the kind of pure golden flame that blazed from the wood of the incense tree... but then he saw a face: kind, wise, unafraid. 'It must be an angel,' he whispered.

Suddenly he strode to the door of the furnace.

'Shadrach! Meshach! Abednego! Come out!'

The three men emerged from the billowing smoke. They were completely unharmed. The angel flickered away.

Nebuchadnezzar was humbled by what he had seen and by the unhesitating faith of Shadrach, Meshach and Abednego. 'May all the world praise your God,' he declared. 'There is no other god who can rescue his faithful people like this.'

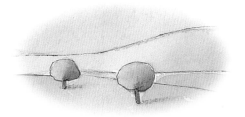

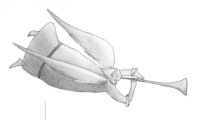

Guardian Angels

*M*ay the bright golden angels
guard me in the encircling fire of God's love.

May the pure silver angels
guide me on the straight path of holiness.

May the glittering jewel angels
open my eyes to the beauty of earth and heaven.

I bind unto myself today
The Power of God to hold and lead,
His eye to watch, his might to stay,
His ear to harken to my need;
The wisdom of my God to teach,
His hand to guide, his shield to ward;
The word of God to give me speech,
His heavenly host to be my guard.

St Patrick (389–461)

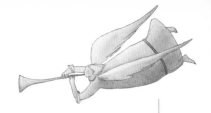

May everything that God has made
join with the angels' story
and tell of God's unfailing love:
give praise and thanks and glory.

*The song of young men in the fiery
furnace, in the Bible book of Daniel*

The Angel Gabriel

One day, God sent the angel Gabriel to earth, to a little town named Nazareth. Its mud-brick houses were clustered on a hilltop above fields and orchards, and in the springtime of the year the warm breezes set the blossom trees fluttering.

Among them sat a young woman named Mary. As she sat enjoying the sunshine and dreaming of her wedding, Gabriel appeared. 'Peace be with you,' said the angel.

Mary started in alarm. 'Do not be afraid,' said Gabriel. 'God has chosen you to give birth to a son, and you will name him Jesus. He will be king of the descendants of Jacob for ever and ever. His kingdom will never end.'

'How can that be?' asked Mary, her voice anxious and disbelieving at the same time. 'I'm a virgin, not yet married.'

'God's power will make all this come true,' replied the angel. 'For this reason, the holy child will be called the Son of God.'

Mary gazed back. The angel, the blossom, the clouds in the sky… suddenly, they all seemed to be part of heaven itself.

'I will do as God wants,' said Mary, humbly. 'May everything happen as you have said.'

Gabriel bowed low, and vanished.

The Angels on the Hillside

Out on the hillside, the shepherds were grumbling.

'Hurry up and get that fire going,' said one. 'It's perishingly cold tonight.' He crouched low against the low stone wall of the sheep fold and drew his cloak close around him.

'If only this wind would quieten down,' replied the second, who was struggling with a heap of glowing embers. 'It keeps blowing the heat out of the fire – and these twigs are wet with frost.'

'It's been a bad winter,' complained the third. 'I'm sure that's why we've had so much trouble with wild animals coming and taking the sheep. Otherwise, we could have taken it in turns to sit out here with the flocks, while the other two of us could have been warm and dry in our homes in Bethlehem.'

'I've hardly made enough income this year to keep myself,' said the first, 'and now there's all this talk about the emperor wanting to put up the amount of tax we have to pay. He's nice and snug in his luxury palace in Rome, and we're sitting on the cold hard ground trying to keep body and soul together.'

'At last – I've got a flame going,' said the second. He stood up wearily. 'We'll need it – see that snow blowing in.'

He went to fetch another meagre bundle of firewood. Just as the fire sprang to life, a sharp gust of wind brought a scattering of snowflakes whirling through the air.

'Here comes the blizzard,' he said. 'I've never seen such snow. It's like the heavens have opened.'

All at once, the crystal flakes were lit with gold. There in the middle of the dark winter night danced an angel, as merry and graceful as a flame of fire.

'Don't be afraid,' said the angel. 'I have good news for you and all the world. Tonight, in Bethlehem, a baby has been born: God's chosen king – the one who will set you free. You will find him – newborn, wrapped in swaddling clothes, and cradled in a manger.'

Then it seemed that each one of the glittering snowflakes unfolded like a flower, and from each an angel flew, dancing and singing.

'Glory to God in the highest; peace on earth,' they sang, and the melody filled the sky and echoed among the stars.

As suddenly as they had come, the angels vanished. The shepherds looked at one another, still dazzled by what they had seen.

'Come on,' said one. 'Let's pile the damp and useless firewood against the gate to keep the wild animals away from the sheep, and then let's get ourselves up the hill and into Bethlehem. We've got to find out if this is true.'

Soon they were hurrying into the town, tiptoeing down alleyways and peering into courtyards.

At last, a tiny point of light led them to a barn. A woman was humming a lullaby; a baby gave a soft cry.

They drew back the cloth that had been fastened over the entrance against the cold.

There was Mary, and Joseph, and a newborn baby.

'This is a miracle,' whispered the shepherds. 'We have just seen a great company of angels who told us we would find this child. He must truly be God's chosen one.'

Mary listened to all they had to say. In her heart, she believed more firmly than ever that her child would be the one to make peace between heaven and earth.

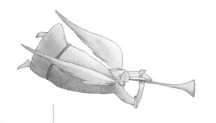

Night-time Angels

*K*eep watch, dear God, with
those who work, or watch, or weep
this night, and give your angels
charge over those who sleep.

St Augustine (354–430)

*I*n the quiet night,
I can hear the wind
that blows from heaven,
bringing life and hope
to all the earth.

The ocean of night is rolling in
over the heavens of blue,
but angels are watching both night and day
and they will take care of you.

My room is dark
in deepest night:
O fill my life
with heaven's light.

I am awake
to unknown fear:
O send the angels
very near.

Lord, keep us safe this night,
Secure from all our fears;
May angels guard us while we sleep,
Till morning light appears.

John Leland (1754–1841)

The Easter Angels

The two women hurried along the path, anxious and fearful. In the pale dawn light each bush and tree seemed to take on a weird and threatening shape.

'Do you think that we will be recognized as followers of Jesus?' asked one. 'Do you think people will want to arrest us like they arrested him? Will we be put to death as he was?'

'It's a worry,' said the other. Her name was Mary Magdalene and she had been one of Jesus' most loyal friends. She glanced over her shoulder and began to walk even more quickly. 'Even so, the danger isn't going to stop us giving Jesus' body a proper funeral. He deserves it: he was such a good person. He only wanted people to know how much God loves them – and then people turned against him. It's so wrong, so unfair.'

For a while they walked on, secretive and silent. They were getting close to the place where Jesus' body had been placed in a tomb. The one who had spoken first had another question.

'How are we going to roll the stone away from the door of the tomb?' she whispered. 'It's too heavy for us, I'm sure.'

Mary Magdalene bit her lip. 'You may be right,' she said. 'I hadn't thought of that.'

All at once, their plans for going back to Jesus' tomb to wrap the body in the traditional way, with precious spices among the cloths, seemed foolish.

'We'll just have to try,' she hissed defiantly. 'Oh no – look! There are Roman soldiers on guard.'

'Now what do we do?' asked the other.

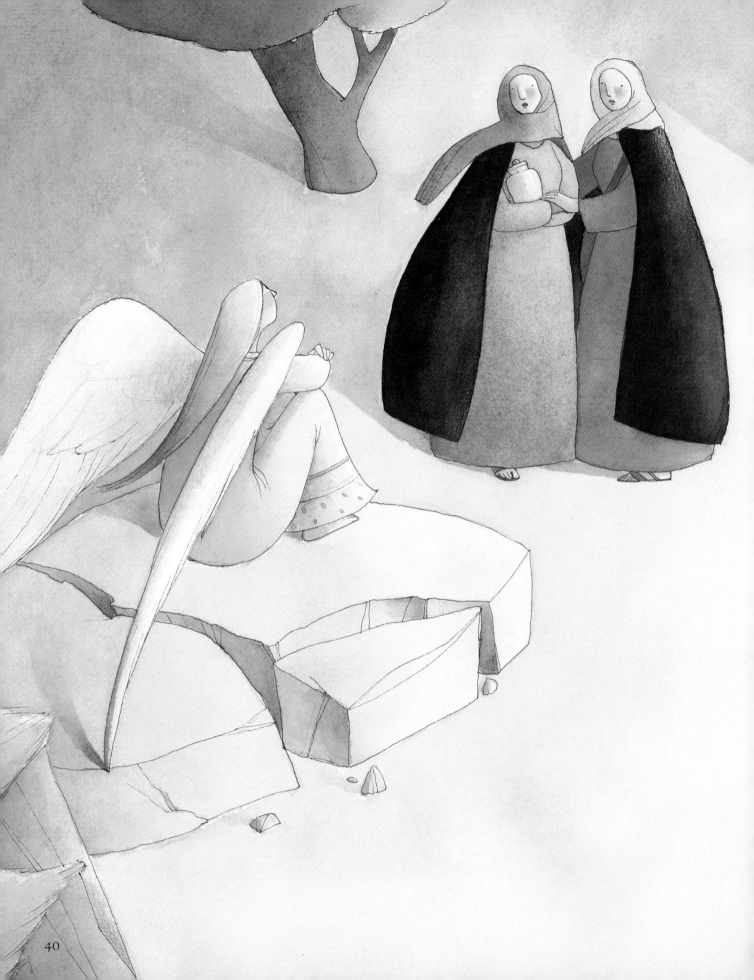

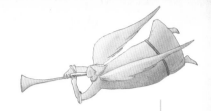

Suddenly there came a low roar like distant thunder: the earth beneath the women's feet trembled; the trees shook and all the birds sped away like dark arrows in a silver sky.

Lightning flashed down and struck the round stone door to the tomb. In the dazzling light, the women saw the soldiers leap to their feet – and then fall down, stunned and unconscious.

The huge door rolled open. The shards of lightning flickered away and there, sitting on the stone, was one of God's angels.

'Don't be afraid,' said the angel to the women. 'I know you are looking for Jesus, who was crucified. He is not here; God has raised him to life. Look – the place where they laid him is empty.

'Go and tell his friends that their beloved Jesus is going to meet them in Galilee.'

The women turned and ran, full of fear and at the same time thrilled with joy.

All at once, the sky was filled with golden light as the sun floated upwards on the eastern skyline. Mary paused for a moment, catching her breath in wonder. It seemed as if she was standing at the door of heaven itself.

The Angel and the Dragon

*H*igh in God's heaven, the ancient dragon awoke and lifted its seven ugly, horned heads. 'The time has come,' it hissed, 'the time to complete what was begun in Eden… the time to destroy all of humankind for ever.'

It flicked its huge, scaly tail, and a third of the stars in heaven sizzled and tumbled down in flames.

As they fell into the pit of darkness, shadows rose up in triumph and began to dance an evil, gleeful dance.

Then a voice rang out, bright and clear as a trumpet. 'You are wrong: the time has come when evil will be destroyed!'

The archangel Michael flew down, his golden sword slicing through the sky. He dealt the dragon a deathly blow, and the monster tumbled through the air.

Behind him, a host of angels swept down on the shadows. The shadows scattered like the scorched and tattered fragments that rise and fall in the smoke of a bonfire.

Then, from the ashes of the great battle between good and evil, there arose a new heaven and new earth. A loud voice called out:

'Now God's home is with humankind once more. They will truly be God's people, as they were in the garden of Eden. Everything that brought grief and sadness is gone. All things have been made anew. Happy are those who come to share the fruit of the tree of life.'

The time had come for angels and humankind to sing together.

43

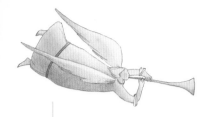

Heavenly Angels

*O*Michael of the angels
And the righteous in heaven,
Shield thou my soul
With the shade of thy wing;
Shield thou my soul
On earth and heaven.

From Carmina Gadelica

*A*s Michael and all the angels
threw the dragon of evil from heaven,
so may I fight evil in the world
with the help of God's holy angels.

*T*hou angel of God who hast charge of me...
Be thou a bright flame before me,
Be thou a guiding star above me,
Be thou a smooth path below me,
And be a kindly shepherd behind me,
Today, tonight, and for ever.

I am tired and I a stranger,
Lead thou me to the land of angels;
For me it is time to go home
To the court of Christ, to the peace of heaven.

From Carmina Gadelica

45

About the Stories and Prayers

Choirs of Angels 8

The Bible contains many mentions of angels who sing God's praise.

The Angel of Paradise 10

This story about the first people, Adam and Eve, comes from the book of Genesis, in the Bible. It tells of how there came to be a great divide between heaven and earth and of the angel who stands at the gateway to paradise.

The Stairway to Heaven 16

This story is about two brothers, Jacob and Esau, and of God's promise to bless the world through Jacob's descendants. It comes from the book of Genesis, in the Bible. This story gives a glimpse of the angels who constantly travel between earth and heaven.

Angels All Around 20

The Bible often speaks of the multitudes of angels whom God made. Unseen or unnoticed, there are angels all around who carry out God's will.

The Angel in the Flames 22

This story is from the book of Daniel, in the Bible. It is set in the court of King Nebuchadnezzar of Babylon. The nation descended from Jacob had become part of his empire and everyone was expected to obey him. This story of three young men who stay loyal to their God tells of a fiery angel who protects them from harm.

Guardian Angels 26

In the Bible, Jesus tells his followers to treat everyone with respect, for even the least important have an angel who takes special care of them.